D0832826

JANET YORK & ROSEMARY CARROLL

PETPOURRI

was a very pampered pup and lived like a king
on a huge estate in the rolling hills of Virginia. He shared his home
with the Hartleys who raised thoroughbred horses.

Corneel liked to watch the horses gallop around the track in the morning mist. When he heard their steady clip clop, clip clop, he knew they were heading back to the stables, and it was feeding time at Tulip Lane Farm.

Mrs. Hartley raised Cavalier King Charles Spaniels just like her most special Cavalier, Corneel. She adored all her dogs and treated them royally, training each with a caring and capable hand. There was Cecile, Madeline, Nikkie, Pippin, Paddy, and all their puppies.

Every dog was special, so it was hard to say goodbye when the time came for the puppies to leave. But Mrs. Hartley was very particular. Her dogs only went to the very best homes with the most loving owners.

On weekdays, Corneel went to school where he practiced obedience and agility. Mrs. Hartley also taught him some funny tricks. He even learned to perform a perfect pirouette and a crazy cross-step. When he danced for the children at the hospital, they would clap their hands and shout, “Do it again, Corneel, do it again.” The doctors and the nurses said, “He’s the best medicine of all.”

On weekends, Mrs. Hartley took her cavaliers to dog shows all over the country. Corneel enjoyed seeing all the other dogs and hearing the crowd cheer as he moved around the ring. Best of all, he almost always brought home a blue ribbon and a silver trophy.

One day, when the leaves
on the sugar maples at
Tulip Lane Farm had turned
to red and gold, Mrs. Hartley
took her cavaliers to the
Friendship Valley
Dog Show in Maryland.
Although it was a long drive,
Corneel didn't mind.
He won two important classes;
the Cavalier Breed Class and The Best in Toy Group.

But before he could compete for the Best in Show,
something terrible happened.

A strange lady, who had been seen at several other shows admiring Corneel, unlatched the dog's kennel and snatched him away.

She shoved him into a cage in the back of her van and barreled out of the parking lot. Corneel bumped his head as they careened around a bend. His little heart pounded. He barked, and he yipped, and he yowled, until his throat was sore.

"Shut up, you stupid dog." Greta Greedly steered her van onto the interstate. "Settle down. It's a long way to New York City."

She reached back and shoved a dog treat through the cage bars. It looked and smelled just like the treats Mrs. Hartley gave him. Corneel snapped it up. It tasted odd and it made him sleepy.

When he awoke, his head felt fuzzy, and his mouth was dry. He whimpered for water.

Greta Greedly sat at a rickety table eating her dinner of meatballs and rice. She plotted as she slurped water from a chipped cup. 'Now all I need is a mate for Corneel. I think I'll hit the Dearborn Show next month. Over 2,000 top quality dogs will be there, and I'll have my pick.'

Corneel whimpered louder. He was so thirsty.

"It's about time you woke up." Greta pushed away from the table and lumbered over to his cage. She clicked open the latch and left the door ajar as she went back to her meal. "Maybe now you'll stop that racket," she muttered.

She skewered a saucy meatball with her fork. "When I make a fortune selling Corneel's pups to the pet stores, I'll eat steak every night."

Corneel eased out of his cage, padded across the peeling linoleum floor, and sat down by the table. He whimpered, again.

"Stop whining. I'll feed you when I'm finished."

Corneel grabbed the edge of the tablecloth and yanked hard. Meatballs bounced to the floor while china shattered and sauce splattered everywhere.

After that, Greta kept Corneel locked in a windowless kitchen that smelled of onions and Brussels sprouts. He was homesick. He had no friends and little exercise. If only he had a squeaky toy to play with or a rubber bone to chew. One afternoon, bored and alone, he pawed at a cabinet door until it popped open. Underneath the kitchen sink, he found a way to have some fun. But someone didn't think it was funny...

"Bad, bad dog!" Greta yelled when she came home and saw what Corneel had done. She grabbed a leather belt to beat him soundly when suddenly the doorbell rang. Annoyed, she turned on her heel and slammed the gate shut… but it failed to lock. Corneel saw his chance to escape. He nosed the gate open…

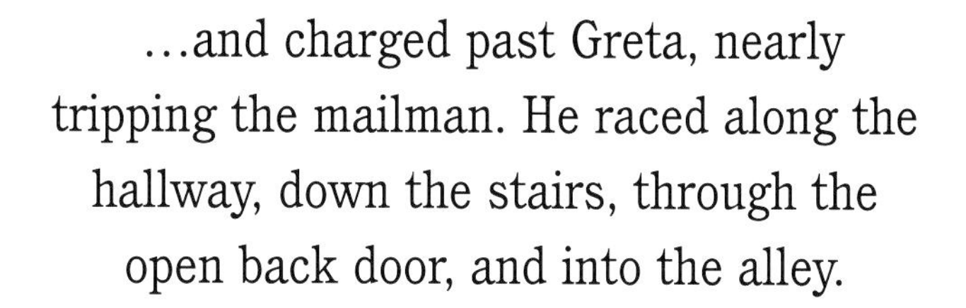

…and charged past Greta, nearly tripping the mailman. He raced along the hallway, down the stairs, through the open back door, and into the alley.

"Stop him! Stop him!" Greta ran after Corneel. "You come back here." Now Greta Greedly had a serious problem. She couldn't report him lost. The police might find out that Corneel was stolen. Huffing and puffing, she chased after him in the icy rain. But the spry little cavalier kept gaining ground. He headed towards a park he'd seen on their short walks. Its sloping lawns and graceful old trees reminded him of home.

"I'll get you!" she yelled. "And when I do, you'll be sorry!"

Corneel skittered across the busy avenue. Horns blared; tires squealed. A garbage truck pelted him with grimy water as he jumped onto the curb. A big bus rumbled by surrounding him in a cloud of exhaust. He coughed and choked and gasped for fresh air.

Cold and scared, Corneel wandered through Central Park. The familiar smell of goats, ponies, cows and chickens at the children's Central Park Zoo made him long for his home. But this wasn't anything like home. Two miserable days later, he was foraging for food in a tipped-over trash can when he heard a whinny. His ears perked. He listened again. The rhythmic clip clop, clip clop grew louder and louder. He heard the jingle of harnesses and the whirr of wheels. ***Horses!*** Corneel raced after them, following the carriages through the park, out onto the street, and around a fancy fountain until they stopped in front of a beautiful building with red-carpeted steps.

On the steps was a boy, named Timothy. He stood outside The Plaza Hotel and waved a silent goodbye. He could feel an emptiness growing inside him as his father's taxi disappeared around the corner. Ever since his mother died a year ago, his dad had stayed close to home. Now he had to go away. Timothy's words of goodbye – along with his tears – were locked in his throat. He wanted to go with his father to Africa. He wanted to help him take pictures and write stories for the news magazine. He didn't want to go to school in New York, and have to make new friends in a strange city.

"It will be an adventure to live at The Plaza Hotel." Timothy's father told him that morning as he helped him unpack. "Why, The Plaza's like a magic castle, and you'll be treated like a prince. Uncle Arthur is absolutely delighted you're staying with him."

Timothy wasn't so sure. Uncle Arthur was a bachelor and the general manager of The Plaza Hotel. He was a very busy man. What was his uncle ever going to do with a nine-year-old boy? He wished that he and his father were back home in the suburbs of Washington, DC.

A rhythmic clip clop, clip clop caught Timothy's attention as two horse drawn carriages pulled up to The Plaza Hotel. Sitting bedraggled beside the carriage was a little dog. Timothy hurried down the steps. The little spaniel hobbled over to him. Timothy extended his hand – palm down. The little dog sniffed, then licked his fingers. When Timothy knelt down to pet him, the dog licked him all over his face. Timothy felt tickly frizzles at the back of his throat.

He gathered the injured dog in his arms and carried him into the hotel. Uncle Arthur would know what to do.

What Uncle Arthur knew were a hundred reasons why they shouldn't take in this stray. But he was worried about his nephew and the pleading look in Timothy's eyes melted his resolve."Very well," he said with a sigh. "We'll notify the proper authorities and take care of the dog until its rightful owner is found. You do understand that we can't keep him?"

Timothy nodded. He understood. But his mother had always said, "Think good things and good things will happen." Maybe…just maybe… the owner would never be found.

Timothy bathed the dog while Uncle Arthur made dozens of phone calls.

They took the stray to see Dr. Callahan. The veterinarian x-rayed the spaniel's injured paw. He listened to his heart and lungs with a stethoscope. He took his temperature and examined his eyes and ears.

"He needs plenty of rest and tender loving care," Dr. Callahan said. "He sprained his paw, and he has a fever. Keep him warm and feed him lightly for the next several days. Boiled chicken and rice would be nice. Be sure to give him his medicine three times a day."

Everyone helped Timothy make the little dog comfortable. Housekeeping brought him a fluffy pillow.

Room service brought him a luscious meal.

Timothy would not leave the dog's side because he knew what it was like to feel lost and alone. He was a very good caregiver. He followed the veterinarian's instructions. He never forgot to give the little dog his medicine and always carried him outside. Soon the little spaniel felt much better. To Uncle Arthur's delight, Timothy seemed better, too.

But the general manager was afraid that his nephew was getting too attached to the dog. He was such a well-trained little pup, and they discovered he could do amazing tricks. Uncle Arthur was certain someone would show up soon to claim him.

In the meantime, Timothy and the little stray grew closer and closer. They snuggled to sleep together.

They got dressed
and brushed their
teeth together.

They played together outside...

inside…

…and up and down.

On his days off, Uncle Arthur took them to see the sights of New York. The Intrepid Sea-Air-Space Museum was like a floating airport. With his trusty copilot, Timothy pretended he was flying to Africa to see his father.

At the American Museum of Natural History, there was so much to see. The dinosaur bones were their favorite.

They shopped at Bloomingdales

...and they stopped at the World's Greatest Toy Store.

They had so much fun; they never wanted to leave.

Weeks passed. Nobody claimed the dog.

Timothy grew happier. He wrote a letter to his father and told him that he liked his new school now, and he'd made some new friends. His best friend helped him mail it.

Uncle Arthur got used to having a little boy and a dog around.
He had to admit that he rather liked it.
And the little lost dog fell in love with his new home.
He brought Uncle Arthur his newspaper every morning and
his slippers every night.

He helped deliver luggage.

He watched the chef whip up biscuits for him and brownies for Timothy's after-school snack.

He welcomed The Plaza's guests...

Corneel endeared himself to one and all.
When guests forgot, he remembered.

"My gloves!" said the elegant lady. "Why I'd lose my head if it weren't attached." She smiled at the Palm Court hostess. "What's his name?"

"We really don't know," said the hostess. "He was a stray. But he spreads so much good will, we just call him our Little Ambassador."

The lovely lady patted the dog's head. "Well then, thank you, Mr. Ambassador, thank you, so much"

Everyone loved the special little spaniel – the bellmen, the desk clerks, the waiters, the concierge, the doormen... They all considered the Little Ambassador a member of The Plaza family.

He fit in so well, he seemed to blend into the scenery.

One Saturday, in the beginning of February, news vans, TV cameras, and reporters lined the street in front of the Plaza. They were there to cover the arrival of the legendary ballerina, Anna Petrova.

Proud of the talented spaniel, Uncle Arthur arranged for the Little Ambassador to present Anna with the keys to The Plaza's Presidential Suite.

The Little Ambassador was charming; his performance, flawless. Lights flashed and cameras clicked. It was all captured live for the five o'clock news. The headlines read: "Petrova Greeted by a Stray Who Came to Stay at The Plaza," and "Pup Performs Perfect Pirouette for the Prima Ballerina."

On the other side of the city, Mrs. Hartley was watching the five o'clock news. She had come to New York City for the Westminster Dog Show. When she saw the stray spaniel on TV, her teacup clattered to the floor. "That's my Corneel!"

Greta Greedly was also watching the five o'clock news as she peeled turnips for her liver stew. "That's Corneel!' The turnip plopped into the sink. "I'll get you now, you little devil, I'll get you now"

Greta Greedly got to The Plaza Hotel first. She skulked into the lobby and hid behind a potted palm until she spied Corneel with a young blond boy. "That's my precious dog," she cried as she approached them. "His name is Corneel. Come to Greta, darling."

The little spaniel growled. His upper lip curled menacingly and he snarled again. Timothy couldn't believe it. His Little Ambassador never ever growled. Greta inched closer. She lunged for the dog. Then she grabbed the dog's leash and pulled hard. "I'll take him home now." Timothy pulled back. "No you won't!" he promised. A tug-of-war began.

Mrs. Hartley arrived at the Plaza just in time to hear Greta's lies. As soon as she saw the little spaniel, she knew he was hers and called out for help. "His name is Corneel, but he's my dog." She pointed an accusing finger. "You are a thief!"

Uncle Arthur arrived with hotel security.
Greta Greedly knew she was in trouble and tried to escape.
Security caught her and held her until the police arrived
and took her away.

Uncle Arthur invited Mrs. Hartley into his office. He suspected the dog's real owner had been found.

"When I saw him on TV, " said Mrs. Hartley, "I knew he was my dog. I called my husband at our farm right away and he faxed the ownership papers to my hotel. You see, Corneel was stolen several months ago from the Friendship Valley Dog Show. Here's his pedigree."

"Hmmm." Uncle Arthur studied the papers. "It looks like The Ambassador… I mean…Corneel is legally yours."

Corneel jumped off the desk and hopped onto the couch next to Timothy. He lay down with his head in Timothy's lap. Timothy's bottom lip started to quiver as he stroked the little spaniel's silky hair. Uncle Arthur dreaded this moment. His nephew looked as sad and lost as he had the day his father left. Uncle Arthur didn't know when it had happened, but he'd fallen in love with the little dog, too.

"When will you be taking him home?" Uncle Arthur asked.

Before Mrs. Hartley could answer, Timothy scooped Corneel up in his arms. "No!" he yelled as he ran from the room. "He's my dog."

Uncle Arthur made a phone call and reassured Mrs. Hartley that they'd be all right. He told her about Timothy – how his mother had died and his father's work had called him away. How his nephew had gently cared for Corneel. How Corneel kept Timothy from being lonely and helped him make friends. "So you might say," Uncle Arthur concluded, "…that the boy saved the dog and the dog saved the boy." Timothy and Corneel were sitting on the stairs near the Grand Ballroom when Uncle Arthur and Mrs. Hartley found them. She sat down next to the tearful boy. Timothy hugged the Little Ambassador to his chest and buried his face in the soft hair.

"You have to go now, Corneel," he whispered. He kissed him on the head then gently placed him in Mrs. Hartley's lap. The little spaniel licked her nose then leaned towards Timothy. Mrs. Hartley understood. She asked Timothy, "Do you love him?" Timothy nodded. "He's the best dog ever." Mrs. Hartley smiled. "Will you take good care of him?" "Yes, of course I will!" said Timothy. He closed his eyes and took a deep breath. He could almost hear his mother say, "Think good things and good things will happen."

Mrs. Hartley lifted Corneel and returned him to Timothy's lap. She could tell that Corneel loved Timothy, too. And she couldn't think of a better place to live than The Plaza Hotel. She scratched the little spaniel behind his floppy ear. "I think you're right, Timothy. Corneel is your dog."

"Yippee!" shouted Timothy as he and Corneel raced down the hall.

To celebrate there was a grand party
given in true Plaza style.
Corneel was officially named
The Young Plaza Ambassador and...

The Plaza

Dear Mrs. Hartley,
Corneel is having a
wonderful summer!
Yesterday we took a
Long walk in the park
then Corneel met a new
friend
skate
write

Mrs. Hartley
Tulip Lane Farm

Uncle Arthur gave him an engraved gold medallion so he'd never be lost again. The scripted words read like a happy ending!

Name: Corneel
Owner: Timothy Brewster
Address: The Plaza Hotel
Fifth Avenue at Central Park South
New York, New York
Title: Young Plaza Ambassador

Mrs. Hartley stayed for the party. When she left, Timothy hugged her and thanked her for her kindness. "I'll write to you all the time," he promised.

Knowing Corneel was in loving hands, Mrs. Hartley returned home to Cecile, Madeline, Nikkie, Pippin, Paddy, and a new litter of puppies. She looked forward to receiving postcards from The Plaza and wondered what adventures awaited Timothy and Corneel.

As for Greta Greedly...

Why, she's on pooper-scooper duty in Central Park.

The End.

Acknowledgements

First, we would like to thank Tim Zagat for our introduction to The Plaza Hotel.

And our sincere gratitude goes to:
Mr. Gary Schweikert and Mr. Tom Civitano at The Plaza Hotel for their personal appearance, kindness, and good will, and also to Lyudmila Bloch for her dedication and hard work.
Ellen Braaf for helping make this story come alive. And to Jeff Kleinman for introducing Ellen to us.
Ann Thornton, Jeff Kozel, the Brewster-York family, the Mallon and Gennarelli families, the Carroll family, the Coppola family, the Williams family, Sean Cummings, and The Plaza Hotel staff for their kind participation in the book.

And finally and most importantly our hugs to Corneel and Mikey Carroll who jumped on beds endlessly, learned new tricks happily, and posed more patiently than most professional models.

It is the intention of the authors to encourage responsible ownership of Cavalier King Charles Spaniels. Your pet will be dependent upon you for its lifetime of up to 15 years.If you are interested in acquiring a Cavalier, or any dog, we suggest that you locate a responsible breeder who sells dogs in good health and of good quality.

For more information about Cavalier King Charles Spaniels or to locate breeders, contact:

American Kennel Club
5580 Centerview Drive, Raleigh, NC 27606-3390
(919) 233-9767 www.akc.org

American Cavalier King Charles Spaniel Club, Inc.
Breed Information Services
www.akcsc.org

Cavalier King Charles Spaniel Club USA, Inc.
Breed Information Services
www.ckcsc.org

Published in the United States by Petpourri Publishers LLC
155 East 72nd Street, New York, NY 10021-4371
Email: Piccadiljy@aol.corn
Printed in Iceland by Oddi Printing
First Edition
2001
ISBN 0-9677177-1-X